THESE DARK HEARTS

A NIX & HARLEIGH PREQUEL

THESE DARK HEARTS: SPECIAL EDITION

A NIX & HARLEIGH PREQUEL

L A COTTON

Published by Delesty Books

THESE DARK HEARTS
A Nix & Harleigh Prequel

Edited by Andrea M Long
Proofread by Sisters Get Lit(erary) Author Services
Cover Designed by Lianne Cotton

DARLING HILL

These Dark Hearts
A Nix & Harleigh Prequel

These Dirty Lies
Nix & Harleigh Book One

These Dead Promises
Nix & Harleigh Book Two

CHAPTER ONE

I'VE NEVER LIKED HALLOWEEN.

There was something disconcerting about the whole thing. Dressing up to be someone—or something—you weren't. Knocking on strangers' doors and asking for candy. It was as if, for those couple of days around October thirty-first, everyone lost their minds.

So yeah, I didn't like Halloween.

But Phoenix, my best friend in the whole world, loved it. Which meant I had to suck it up, because when it came to Halloween celebrations nobody did it quite like Nix and his guys, and they never left me out.

Ever.

"Yo, Birdie." Stones pelted my window and I

smiled, stretching my arms above my head, my toes curling as I shook off the lingering thrall of sleep.

"Ten minutes," Nix yelled from beyond the window of my small bedroom in the double-wide I'd lived in my whole life.

"Ten minutes," I shouted back, my smile growing. He always said ten minutes, but I always took at least twenty.

I wasn't a morning person. I preferred the night. Something about the quiet of the dark. Nix said I had affinity to the darkness, which highly amused him considering how much I loathed Halloween.

Gingerly climbing out of bed, I tamed my dark hair into a ponytail and slipped into my closet-sized bathroom to wash up.

Years ago, the smell of bacon would have filled the air. Or maybe pancakes and syrup. But those days were long gone. Now, if I didn't get my own breakfast there was no one to make it for me.

My heart squeezed at the thought.

She's still here, I reminded myself. But it wasn't the same. The light had long gone out in my mom's eyes. Now she was nothing more than a shell. Empty and hollow.

Inhaling a deep breath, I braced myself for whatever state she was in, and made my way into the living room. "Mom?" I called out.

Trepidation skittered up my spine as I approached her bedroom door on the other side of the trailer. "Mom, are you awake?"

Peeking inside, I was hit with a wave of relief at the sight of her fragile form curled up in bed, sleeping. But it was tinged with disappointment and anger when my eyes landed on the empty bottle of vodka turned over on her nightstand.

I grabbed a bowl from the kitchen and placed it next to her, rolling her onto her side as best I could. I'd found her one too many times choking on her own vomit to not take precautions. It was second nature now.

By the time I was done, I had five minutes to spare to grab a granola bar and some juice. It wasn't exactly the breakfast of champions, but it wasn't like I had much of an appetite these days anyway.

I'd just reached the door, when Nix's shadow flickered across the window.

"Morning." I grinned stepping out onto the wraparound deck. When I'd been just a little girl, I'd thought we were lucky to have one of the biggest trailers in the whole of Darling Row.

How wrong I'd been.

"Get over here." Nix pulled me into his arms, hugging me tight and I melted into his sturdy hold.

If Mom was the storm in my life, unpredictable

and tumultuous, Nix was the sun. Constant and true, he never let me down. He was my best friend, my protector, my confidante, and growing up, he'd been the big brother I'd never had.

But lately, something had changed between us. His touch made my skin a little too tight, and his smile made my stomach flutter like a thousand butterflies taking flight.

We weren't kids anymore. We were juniors now, both seventeen. I had boobs and hips and an ass, and Nix had muscles in places I didn't realize guys could develop muscles. If he noticed the changes in my body, he didn't let on, and I didn't know whether to be relieved or bitterly disappointed.

Because I didn't want things to change between us.

I didn't.

Even if I was hopelessly, irrevocably in love with Phoenix Wilder.

"HEY, NIX." Cherri Jardin strolled over to him as we climbed out of his beat down Corolla. She paid me no attention, but that was nothing new.

When you were best friends with a guy like Nix, you quickly got used to girls' hostility or downright his arm over my shoulder. Instantly, some of the fire inside me died out. "Not a fan of Cherri?" he asked.

I glanced up at him and rolled my eyes. "I don't know what you see in her."

"If you have to ask, you're not ready to know the answer." His expression was teasing but it only made the knot in my stomach tighter.

"I'm not eleven anymore, Nix." I shucked out of his hold, hating the way my cheeks burned under his scrutiny.

Hurrying away from him, I was hardly surprised when he grabbed my arm and yanked me back. "What's going on with you?"

Tell him.

I could tell him and what… hope he returned my affections when I knew he didn't feel the same? I was his best friend. The girl he'd placed neatly in the friend zone years ago.

No, I couldn't tell him. Nix was my best friend. His friendship meant too much to risk it on a silly case of unrequited love.

I just had to ignore my growing feelings, the sense of possessiveness I felt over him, and eventually, it would go away, and things could go back to how they'd always been between us.

"Wren," he said, preferring to use my middle name. "Talk to me."

"I…"

Tell him.

Just tell him.

No, don't tell him.

Don't ever tell him.

"I'm worried about Mom." I let out a weary breath. "She's been worse than usual lately. It makes me… jittery."

"Shit, babe. Come here." He pulled me into his arms as if it was the most natural thing in the world.

And it was.

Everything about the way he held me felt right. It felt… destined. As if we were inevitable.

But there would always be a glaring wall between us because my feelings for him weren't platonic anymore.

They hadn't been for years.

"I'm fine." I pushed him away gently, smiling. "I always feel uneasy this time of year."

"Seriously, B, you need to get over your fear of Halloween." He gave me a crooked smile.

"I'm not scared, jerk face." I stuck my tongue out at him. "It's just… you know all the costumes and unnecessary mayhem gives me the heebie jeebies." Trading some textbooks in my locker, I took a second to catch my breath.

He knew.

He knew something was wrong between us.

God, this was the worst thing that could happen.

"You're still coming to the party, right?"

The party that the kids from our neighborhood threw down at the reservoir every year.

"Nix." His name caught in my throat like a lover's sigh. "I don't know…"

"But you have to come."

"Why?" I peeked up at him through my long lashes. I hadn't meant to ask, but now the word was hanging between us, and I realized I needed to know.

I needed to know why it was so important to him that I was there.

"Why?" A ripple went through the air, my skin growing tight again as he studied me. His brows drew together, his gunmetal gray eyes swirling with darkness. His thumb pressed gently into his bottom lip as the silence stretched before us.

But then someone yelled down the hall and the spell was broken. Nix blinked, that easy smile of his fixing back into place.

"Why?" He chuckled. "Because I wouldn't be much of a best friend if I let you stay home and watch *Friends* reruns, would I?"

I loosened the breath I was holding.

For a second, for one single beat in time, I'd thought he was going to say something else entirely.

Dejection rose inside me like a tidal wave, devastating and unrelenting, and I had to glance away to try and school my disappointment.

"Come on, B, it'll be fun." He reached for me, twirling a strand of my hair around his finger. Always touching me the way guys touched their girlfriends. A brush of his hand against mine. Crushing me in a bear hug. Dropping a kiss on my head or cheek.

Nix wasn't afraid of human contact. He sought it out. It just didn't mean the same thing when he touched me as when he touched girls like Cherri.

My heart cinched.

I'd watched him for years flirt and make out in darkened corners of parties or behind the bleachers. Nix loved kissing, he loved sex. I'd heard him talk to the guys about it enough. And it had never bothered me because I knew I had the one thing they never would.

His heart.

Phoenix Wilder loved me.

He loved me with everything he was.

He just didn't love me enough.

CHAPTER TWO

DARLING ROW, OR THE ROW AS EVERYONE CALLED IT, was the vast trailer park on the edge of Darling Hill, a small town nestled in the Hudson Valley right between Albany and Hudson.

The place where dreams came to die, or at least that's what my mom liked to call it whenever she was sober enough to hold down a real conversation.

She'd grown up across the nice side of town, Old Darling Hill. Where money was no object and kids didn't have to worry about where their next meal was coming from. But when she'd gotten pregnant with me at the tender age of nineteen to a man seven years her senior, she was exiled from her family. My family.

So she'd moved out to The Row and started over. A young woman with a baby on the way and nothing but the clothes on her back. My father—or sperm donor as he more rightfully deserved to be called—paid her off. He gave her enough money to make ends meet and washed his hands of us.

Anger flashed inside me as I sat on the deck, sipping my warm milk.

I'd only ever known this.

The rows and rows of trailers. Air thick with desperation and tainted with the aftertaste of shattered dreams. It could be worse, I knew that. But it was a bitter pill to swallow knowing that if things had been different, that if my sperm donor had loved her as much as she'd loved him, I would have been one of the rich kids attending Darling Academy.

A bitter laugh escaped my lips.

I couldn't imagine ever being one of them, with their expensive cars and designer labels and boutique stores.

Kids from this side of town rarely ventured past the reservoir. It was the boundary line separating Old Darling Hill with our neighborhood that ran north along the Hudson River.

Occasionally, kids from the academy wandered into our territory, but it never usually ended well for anyone.

"Harleigh, baby, you out there?" Mom's gravelly voice drifted from inside.

"Yeah, Mom, I'm out here." I drained the rest of my milk and braced myself.

She appeared in the door, thin and pale, her hair as unkempt as her clothes. "There you are, baby." She smiled, revealing liquor-stained teeth.

"What's up, Mom?"

"Just wanted to see how you're doing, sweetheart. I missed you today."

"You were out cold when I left." I arched a brow, wondering if she would confess to the empty bottle of vodka.

Of course, she didn't.

Because her addiction was something we didn't talk about. The huge fucking elephant in the room.

"It was a bad night." Shame washed over her, and she dropped her gaze. "Did Nix give you a ride to school?"

"You know he did, Mom." *He's given me a ride every morning since he got his driver's license.*

"He's good to you. But I worry, Harleigh. Nix and his friends are—"

"Don't." I jumped up, ready to go to bat for the only person who had ever given a crap about me.

"Sweetheart, I just—"

"No." I snapped. "You don't get to do that. You don't get to act like you care when you've barely been sober since the semester started." Which was weeks ago.

Her expression guttered as she inhaled a deep breath. "I'm trying, baby. I just worry. You're… you're such a good girl, Harleigh, baby. And Nix is… there's something dark inside that boy. I can feel it."

Strangled laughter bubbled in my chest. "Yeah well, newsflash, Mom. There's darkness in me too."

She reared back like I'd physically slapped her. "D-don't say that, don't ever say that."

"Whatever, Mom." Brushing past her, I slipped into the trailer, but she followed, staggering after me like a wraith moving in the shadows.

"Harleigh Wren, please, baby, I don't want to fight."

I whirled around and glared at her. "What do you want then? Because you sure as hell don't want to know how my day went or whether I'm keeping up my grades or eating right or—"

"Stop." She cried, rubbing her clavicle. "Please, stop."

"Well, what, Mom? What do you want, huh?"

Sometimes, it was easier to deal with her when she was drunk than deal with… with this. Her lame attempt at pretending she cared when she hadn't bothered asking for weeks if I had enough money to buy groceries or school supplies or to replace the worn contents of my bare-minimum closet.

"It's Halloween and I know you usually go out with Nix and—"

"Seriously, Mom. You managed to drag yourself out of bed to warn me about the party."

Unbelievable.

"I've been going out on Halloween with Nix for years."

"I know, baby. I know. But you're not a child anymore, Harleigh. You're all grown up and… and I worry."

"Oh, please. You're a little late to talk to me about the birds and bees, Mom."

The blood drained from her face as she spluttered, "You mean… you and Nix…"

"What?" My cheeks burned. "No. God, no."

Relief washed over her, but I didn't have the heart to tell her I was flushed for entirely different reasons.

Because now all I could think about was being with Nix like that. Our bodies pressed closed, slick with sweat. The sound of our moans in the darkness. The feel of him moving on top of me.

I squeezed my eyes shut, forcing myself to take a deep breath.

"Harleigh, baby?" Mom's voice cracked with

regret. But it was always the same. She pulled herself out of her drunken stupor long enough to berate me and then went back to her old ways.

She'd never liked Nix. Part of me thought she was jealous because he was the person I turned to. But it wasn't like I'd ever been able to lean on her.

"Look, Mom," I sighed, hating the confrontation. "Nix is my best friend. He's been there for me." *He's still there for me.* "I know you don't like him, but I need him."

"I know, sweetheart. I know. I just… I don't want you to waste your last couple of years at high school in his shadow." She came over, grabbing my hand in hers. Her bony fingers clutched onto me like a life raft. "You could do anything you want, baby. Be anything you want."

"Mom…"

"Just promise me you'll always chase your dreams, Harleigh. Go after what *you* want."

"Sure, Mom." I fought the urge to roll my eyes. "Whatever."

"You're such a good girl, baby. I'm so proud of you."

Proud of me?

She sure had a funny way of showing it.

I WAS APPLYING the last of my makeup when my cell phone pinged.

Nix: Trick or treat?

Me: Haha, very funny. I'm almost ready.

Nix: Good, I'm ready to fuck things up.

I rolled my eyes at that. Nix didn't need an excuse to fuck things up, he lived for chaos.

He and his two closest friends, Zane and Kye, were well known around Darling Hill. They liked to party, live life on the wild side, and generally fuck with the establishment.

Their words, not mine.

It had never bothered me before. They usually kept me out of their mayhem and Nix would never put me in harm's way. But after my argument with Mom, I couldn't shake the feeling that something was different.

I knew I was different—I was having all these lusty feelings for Nix—but there was something else circling. A shift in the air.

Or maybe I just needed to relax and have one night of good old-fashioned teenage fun.

Staring at myself in the mirror, I snorted. Nix

was going to die when he saw my costume choice this year. The Harley Quinn outfit was the sexiest thing I'd ever worn, but when I'd spotted it in the local Goodwill store, I'd bought it on a whim.

Maybe, deep down, I'd bought it to try to get Nix to notice me.

Everyone went all out for the party, especially the girls. Slutty zombie brides, sexy angels, seductive devils; the guys always had a field day. And I usually blended in with the shadows, opting for something more reserved. Because I wasn't *that* girl.

But maybe I could be tonight.

My cell phone pinged again, and I smiled.

Nix: Your chariot awaits.

He was such a dork.

Only for you. I silenced the little voice.

It was true. Not many people got to see the side Nix saved just for me. But it seemed like a fair trade when I didn't get to see the side reserved for the girls in his life.

My fingers trembled as I texted him back, nervous energy bouncing around in my stomach. "Relax." I inhaled a sharp breath. "You've got this."

I looked hot. I looked like the type of girl Nix usually hooked up with. The blue and red skirt sat high on my thighs and the white cropped tee revealed my flat stomach. I'd curled my hair and pulled it into two high pigtails. My black boots had seen better days, but they would have to do, and they looked killer teamed with my white, knee-high socks.

God, was I really doing this?

I sucked my bottom lip between my teeth, trying to imagine Nix's reaction. A soft laugh of disbelief spilled from my lips. He was going to freak when he saw me.

Especially after I'd hinted that I didn't want to go. But watching him with Cherri, and then hearing my mom tell me to always go after what I wanted… well, it had flipped a switch inside me.

She was right.

This life wouldn't hand me my dreams. I had to chase them. Grab them with both hands and make them happen.

And the thing I wanted most in the world? Nix.

For once, I wanted him to look at me the way he looked at them. I wanted nothing more than to affect him the way he affected me.

Another text came through and I quickly read it.

Nix: Kye is getting restless… are you coming?

Me: Leaving now.

I grabbed the few dollars I'd saved from watching our neighbors' kids and stuffed them in my purse along with my lip gloss and cell phone. Then I slung it over my body and went to check on Mom.

"I'm leav—"

Disappointment washed over me as I took in her sleeping form, curled up on the couch, fingers still loosely curled around another bottle of vodka.

The irony wasn't lost on me. The refrigerator was always bare, the cupboards filled with nothing but packets of ramen noodles and stale crackers. But she could always find enough money to buy her beloved liquor.

"See you later, Mom," I murmured as I reached the front door, and stepped out into the inky night.

"HOLY. Shit. Is that little Harleigh Wren Maguire under all... that?" Kye let out a low whistle as I climbed into Nix's car.

"Hey, guys." My stomach churned as I tugged on the hem of my skirt, fully aware of how revealing it was.

"Birdie," Nix whispered thickly, his eyes roaming

over my body. His hands curved around the steering wheel, gripping it tightly.

"What do you think?" I asked, peeking over at him sheepishly.

"I… it's…" He cleared his throat. "It's a little… much, don't you think?"

A little much?

My heart withered in my chest.

"Dude." Kye leaned over from the back seat and hit Nix upside the head. "A little much? Have you lost your goddamn mind? She looks hot as—ow, fuck face, what the hell was that for?"

"We should go," Nix grumbled, revving the engine.

So much for impressing him. He thought I looked stupid.

Why was I even surprised?

Nix didn't think of me as anything more than a little sister. Someone he had to protect and look out for. Someone he let tag along because he felt sorry for her.

I pressed my head against the cool glass, trying to catch my breath. Trying not to let the torrent of emotion crashing inside of me break free.

Don't cry. Don't you dare cry.

"I heard that some of the academy kids might show," Zane said.

"Nah, no way." Nix shifted.

I didn't look at him. I couldn't. Not after his flippant comment had shredded my heart into tiny, jagged pieces. But I felt the animosity rolling off him. There were few things he hated more than the kids that lived across town.

"They don't have big enough balls. Especially not after how we kicked their asses on the field last month."

"Only telling you what I heard, man."

"If they're stupid enough to wander into our territory, then they'd better be ready to pay the price."

"Hell yeah." Zane leaned forward, chuckling, and the two of them high-fived through the seats.

The three of them were dressed in their usual plain black hoodies and black jeans, but tonight, they'd added scary LED neon masks. Nix wasn't wearing his, but Kye and Zane were, and the effect was oddly chilling. But then I couldn't see their eyes, and eyes told you so much about a person.

Like when I peeked over at Nix and his gaze collided with mine. Cold and stormy, swirling with disapproval. His jaw clenched as he sucked in a sharp breath and refocused his attention on the road.

"Nix, I—"

"Not now, B, yeah. Not now."

I sunk lower in the seat, wishing it would swallow me whole.

Tonight was supposed to bring us closer together, to make him realize that I wasn't a kid anymore.

But in that moment, he'd never felt more distant.

CHAPTER THREE

Darling Hill Reservoir was a local hotspot with the kids from our neighborhood. Everyone who was anyone had spent at least a summer or two down here, swimming in the murky blue waters, sunbathing on the shady banks. Surrounded by the dense forest, it was the perfect place for teenagers to come and let loose without upsetting the authorities.

Tonight, it had been turned into party central. A huge bonfire licked the night sky as people danced and laughed, sipping warm beer and liquor stolen from their parents' drinks cabinets.

"Wilder, about time." Paul Odell sauntered over to us, fist bumping the guys. "Shit, Harleigh, is that you under all—"

"Don't go there, man," Kye mumbled. "Not unless you want Nix to rip your head off."

Paul stepped back, smirking as he held up his hands. "I can see why it would be a problem." He glanced at me again and then back to Nix. "Shit, man." He chuckled as if they were sharing a private joke.

But it only made the knot in my stomach tighten.

Nix had barely said two words to me on the ride over, and it was starting to piss me the hell off.

So he didn't like my costume. He didn't have to be an ass about it.

"I'm going to get a drink," I said, leaving them talking about whatever guys talked about.

You know what they talk about, girls like Cherri.

Nix didn't follow.

And part of me wished I didn't want him to.

A couple of guys watched me as I wandered over to the collection of beer coolers and swiped a bottle but the second I met their stares, they glanced away. It was always the same whenever I partied with Nix. No one looked at me, no one talked to me… no one except—

"Chloe," I said, dropping down on the bench beside her. "You came."

"Dumb, right? I mean, Kye will probably kill me when he realizes. But screw him. I'm sixteen. He was partying way before that."

My lips curved. Chloe Carter was a handful.

Strong-willed, sassy, and she took no shit from her brother or his friends. But unlike me, she was the kind of girl who navigated the social hierarchy of high school.

"I like your outfit," I said, studying her Catwoman get up.

"This old thing." She flashed me a grin. "It was my seventh-grade costume for the contest at school. I had to alter it a little to fit but I'm pleased with how it came out."

"You look amazing."

"You don't look so bad yourself, Harley Quinn." She smirked. "Now all you need is to find your Joker." Her laughter barely penetrated me as I found Nix across the bonfire, laughing and talking with a group of sexy angels. But one of them drew my eye more than the others.

Cherri.

My heart cinched.

"You know, you could just tell him how you feel." Chloe nudged my shoulder with hers.

"I don't know what you mean."

"Sure, you don't." She rolled her eyes. "You've been in love with him your whole life."

"I..." I was pretty sure my cheeks were on fire.

"It's okay, I won't tell anyone. I mean, I get it. It's

Nix. You two have that special bond. Childhood friends turned lovers. It's cute."

"He doesn't see me like that." The words were like ash on my tongue.

"He'd have to be dumb not to notice."

"You mean like you and Maddox," I said, following her line of sight to where Maddox West stood with his friends. A group of them dressed as zombie football players.

"It's not like that between us. Maddox is… he's kind of an asshole."

I chuckled at that. I knew all about assholes, especially ones with dark hair and molten eyes and tattoos that screamed bad boy.

But Nix had never been an asshole, not to me.

Not until tonight.

"I don't know how you stand it," Chloe's voice lowered. "Watching him with them."

Her words made me look over at Nix and the guys again. Cherri had moved closer, pressing her double Ds into his arm as she gazed up at him, all seduction and sin.

My stomach dropped. "I… I'm used to it."

"Yeah, well, he's a fool for not realizing what's right in front of him."

"Thanks."

A sticky trail of dejection snaked through me.

"Look at us." Chloe stood, brushing her hands down her skintight latex shorts. "It's Halloween. The night itself is built on mischief and mayhem and we're sitting here all mopey. Let's go, Maguire."

"G-go?"

"Yeah." She rolled her eyes. "To get a drink, dance… find some cute guys to talk to. Anything but sit here like this." Hurt flashed into her eyes as she glanced back over to where Maddox was. "What do you say?"

Chloe held out her hand to me, and I peeked over at Nix again. His arm was around Cherri now as they laughed. His lips dusted her ear, the slender curve of her neck.

Damn you, Phoenix Wilder.

"Let's go," I said, with an air of confidence I didn't really feel.

But she was right. I couldn't stay here and let my heart break any more than it already had. Besides, Nix was my ride home.

I was stuck here now.

Whether I wanted to be or not.

"THIS IS FUN, RIGHT?" Chloe yelled over the music as we danced to the heavy beat pounding through the air. My skin was slick with sweat, my heart racing with every roll of my hips and swing of my arms.

She was right, it was fun.

The couple of drinks she'd snagged us helped.

But then my eyes landed on Nix across the bonfire, and everything closed in around me. I inhaled sharply, watching like some kind of masochist as he hooked his arm around Cherri and pulled her into his side. She giggled, draping her arm around his neck and throwing her head back letting him lick her skin. Kiss her. Bite her.

Heat bloomed in my stomach, but it wasn't only hate swirling there. It was something else. Something dark and needy. A deep pulse inside me. A pulse that only quickened when his eyes locked on mine. Nothing else existed. Not Chloe or the music or the wild flames dancing against the inky backdrop.

There was only me and Nix.

The boy who owned my heart even if he didn't want it.

And her.

She was part of this, whether she realized it or not.

Cherri straddled his long, outstretched legs and started dancing, grinding on him as if he belonged to her.

He didn't.

Nix was mine.

Only he wasn't, not in all of the ways that counted.

Nix didn't take his eyes off me, yet he let her kiss him, touch him, take what wasn't hers to take.

Why?

Why are you doing this?

Raw emotion stabbed at me. Deep and visceral, it shredded what was left of my heart wide open. But I couldn't stop watching. I couldn't stop silently asking him why?

"Harleigh." Chloe grabbed my arm, trying to pull me away. "Don't do this to yourself. He's not worth it."

But he was.

Nix was everything to me—*everything.*

So why was he being such an asshole?

Tears stung my eyes and I blinked, breaking the volatile connection between us. "I need some air."

"Girl." Chloe chuckled. "We're in the middle of bumfuck nowhere."

"You know what I mean." I stumbled toward the reservoir where it was quieter, the crowds of kids all looking to party sticking closer to the bonfire.

"Harleigh, wait," she called after me, but I

couldn't stop. I needed to get away from her, from them.

From myself.

What had I been thinking wearing this stupid outfit and thinking I could impress him?

Nix didn't see me like that.

He'd never seen me like that.

I was his little Birdie. His best friend. The girl he would always love but never want.

God, it hurt.

"Hey, you okay?" Chloe nudged me gently, lacing her arm through mine.

"I'm… I'm stupid."

"No, you're not. But you know, maybe you should just tell him how you really feel. At least it'll be out there and you can move on, one way or another…"

"So he can reject me with words too? No thanks." Strangled laughter almost choked me. I leaned into her, grateful that I wasn't alone.

Chloe and I weren't best friends or anything like that, but she was the nearest thing I had to a girl-friend. I could talk to her about this stuff, couldn't I?

"I know we're not close or anything," she went on. "But I'm always here, Harleigh. If you need a friend—" Something caught her attention along the beach and her eyes widened. "Oh shit," she breathed, and my head snapped over to whatever she had seen.

"Is that—"

"Marc Denby and his crew, yeah."

We both watched Marc and his friends stroll toward the party as if they owned the place.

They didn't.

They were from across town, Old Darling Hill, and they definitely didn't belong in a place like this.

"Why would they come here?" I whispered.

"Why do you think?" She cast me a grim look. "Come on. We should go see what's happening. Kye can't get in trouble again. He'll get kicked off the team."

So would Nix.

The Darling Hill High Hawks were on a winning streak; partly because Nix and Kye ran an impressive offence and partly because most other teams feared them.

Chloe dragged me back toward the bonfire. Marc and his friends had already reached the party, people giving them a wide berth.

"You must be lost," Nix said, stepping forward, his LED mask pushed up onto his head and Cherri now nowhere in sight. "Because I know you didn't come here willingly."

Kye and Zane flanked him, the three of them like a wall of muscles and ink and intimidation.

"It's a free country, Wilder." Marc spat, grabbing his ball cap and spinning it backwards before lowering it back. As if that one move somehow made him any kind of match for Nix.

It didn't.

I knew that.

Marc knew that.

The whole goddamn crowd knew that. But guys were stupid, and they liked fighting.

Especially Darling Hill High and Darling Academy.

"You fucked us over at the game."

"Still crying about that, Denby?" Nix snorted. "You came to the wrong place if you're looking for sympathy."

"You're a fucking asshole, you know that, right?" Marc took a step closer, a ripple of anticipation going through the air.

From the clench of his fists at his sides it was clear he hadn't turned up to bury the hatchet.

"Guy has a death wish," Chloe muttered, grabbing my hand and pulling me around the back of the crowd toward where her brother and Nix were standing. But an arm shot out, yanking me to the side.

"What do we have here?" a voice said, his eyes widening with recognition. "I know you."

"Doubtful," I hissed.

"No, I do. You're Wilder's pet." The guy's eyes skated down my body, lighting up with dark intentions. A violent shudder went through me.

"Get your hands off her, douchebag." Chloe burst through the crowd.

"Not a chance, hot stuff. Denby will be pleased to see you." He tightened his hold on me and shoved me toward the front of the crudely formed circle.

Everyone was looking now.

Looking at Nix and Marc… and me.

I dared not glance in Nix's direction, but I felt his glare, burning into the side of my face.

"And what do we have here?" Marc drawled, giving me the once over. His friend leaned in, whispering something about *Wilder's pet*.

I hated that nickname—hated that's what they thought about me.

Hated even more that they were right.

Nix didn't want me. He didn't see me as his girlfriend or even his friend-with-benefits. I was his best friend, sure. But people outside our group—him, Kye, Zane, and me—didn't really get it. And it had never bothered me.

Until now.

Until the whispers started like a slow wave rolling toward shore. I heard Cherri and her friends snickering, their cruel words and taunts rising above the rumble of voices.

Is that Harleigh... little Harleigh Maguire?

What is she wearing?

Wilder's pet... sounds about right, the way she follows them around like a lost puppy.

It's tragic, she's tragic.

Everybody knows Nix isn't a one girl kind of guy.

I'd never been at the center of their attention before, not like this. Because Nix protected me. He kept the wolves at bay, warning off anyone who dared speak ill of me.

But not tonight.

Tonight, Nix just stood there, doing nothing.

Plunging the knife deeper into my heart.

CHAPTER FOUR

"Let go of me," I hissed, thrashing against Marc's hold.

If Nix wasn't going to save me, I'd damn well save myself.

But just as I was about to do something stupid, like knee Marc in the balls, Kye stepped forward. "Ballsy move, Denby. Harleigh belongs to us."

Not him.

Not Nix.

Us.

Any other time, the words would have warmed my soul, but not tonight. Tonight, they rang loud and clear in my mind as 'not Nix's.'

I blinked back a fresh wave of tears.

"Funny, I thought she was Wilder's pet. Or maybe

you all share. Maybe she gets on her knees like a good little slut for all three—"

"Enough," Nix growled, taking a single step forward, the ground shaking beneath his boots. Yet he still didn't look at me.

And that single inaction cut me deeper than anything else.

Why can't you look at me?

"What do you really want, Denby? Surely, even you know you're starting something you can't finish."

"You think you're so fucking untouchable." Marc squeezed my bicep, the skin smarting underneath his cruel touch. "The mighty Phoenix Wilder, scared of nothing and no one."

"When you've got nothing to lose it's easy not to give a shit." Nix shrugged, flashing that easy smile of his. The one he often wore. But I knew it was a front. A mask. A façade.

Nix cared. He just didn't like people to know.

Still, it didn't stop his words from hitting me dead in the chest.

"Interesting." Marc pulled me flush against his chest, dipping his lips to my ear. "Maybe Wilder won't mind if I—"

"Don't you ever get tired of listening to yourself?" Zane slipped his mask off, swaggering toward us, a dark glint in his eyes. Where Nix was the leader, and Kye was the joker, Zane was the unpredictable one. A quiet mercurial storm. When he waded into a situation, things usually ended in violence.

But he didn't scare me. Maybe it was the way he'd always been the silent protector in my life. Watching over me and Nix in equal measure.

Or maybe I just had a thing with boys and dark hearts. Because if Nix kept his heart locked away, Zane kept his buried under six feet of ice.

"Oh look, it's the—"

"Come here, Harleigh," Zane said, beckoning me toward him.

I tried to move but Marc tightened his hold on me. "Not so fast."

"You're playing a dangerous game, Denby." Zane glowered, his eyes as dark as the night. A shiver ran through me. He looked deadly. A cold deadly tempest waiting to strike.

"Just tell them, man." Marc's friends urged.

"Tell us what?" Nix asked, still not looking at me.

"We want a rematch. Hawks versus Devils."

"A rematch?" Laughter filled the air. "We beat you fair and square."

"On your field. We all know if you and your guys come down to our field it'll be a different story."

Nix narrowed his eyes, studying Marc with unnerving attention.

"So, what's it gonna be, Wilder?"

"And we can just walk into your school, no questions asked?"

"Consider it handled."

Chloe muttered something under her breath. Probably what a stupid idea it was. If Nix and the team went anywhere near Darling Academy, there would be trouble.

Everyone knew that.

Everyone including Nix.

But when has that ever stopped him before?

"Name the date and time and we'll be there."

"Next weekend, bye week." Marc sounded smug as if he knew Nix was a foregone conclusion. And maybe he was. "Saturday night at eight."

Nix gave him an imperceptible nod, his eyes finally flicking to mine. But I felt none of his usual warmth. In fact, his piercing gaze chilled me to the bone. "Now if you want to walk out of here in one piece, let her go."

"She's all yours." Marc kissed my cheek before shoving me forward. Hard.

I lost my footing, stumbling.

"Harleigh!" Chloe yelled, but it was too late. I was

falling. Down, down, down as snickers rang out around me.

"Fuck," someone breathed, right as strong arms caught me.

For a second, I thought it was Nix, but when my gaze lifted, Zane was the one staring down at me.

"You good?" he clipped out, helping me back to my feet. I nodded, too embarrassed to reply. "You know, maybe—"

"Motherfucker," Kye yelled, and I turned back just in time to see him collide with one of Marc's friends.

The two of them crashed to the ground in a blur of fists. "You ever look at my sister again and I'll fucking kill you."

Kye got the upper hand, pinning him as he drove his fist into the guy's nose. A sickening crunch reverberated through the air, blood spraying everywhere.

"Kye, stop!" Chloe tried to haul her brother off the guy. "Stop, you idiot."

"Fuck." Zane released me, jogging over to Kye. He yanked him away from the guy who was groaning in pain, clutching his broken nose.

"What the hell, Kye?" Chloe started wailing on her brother.

"He fucking looked at you like—"

"You broke his nose because he looked at me? Seriously? What the hell is wrong with you?"

"You won't get away with this, Carter," Marc seethed, helping his injured friend to his feet.

"With what? All I saw was your friend trip and smash his face on the ground." Nix shrugged, wearing an amused smirk. "Now if you don't want the same thing to happen to you, I suggest you run along back to your side of town."

Everyone held their breath, waiting to see what Marc would do. But reason got the better of him, because he and his friends stalked off back toward the woods.

Nix walked over to a cooler and swiped a bottle of beer, uncapping it and thrusting it in the air. "It's Halloween," he bellowed. "Let's get fucked up."

The place erupted, everyone cheering and whistling. Beers went flying, drinks spraying in the air like a sheet of rain. Girls shrieked and guys high-fived.

The party had officially started, and I wanted nothing but to escape.

"Oh my God, Harleigh." Chloe came rushing over to me. "Are you okay?"

"I'm fine."

I wasn't, not by a long shot, but she didn't need to know that.

"Listen," I said. "Can I get a ride back with you later?"

"Sure." Her gaze snagged on something over my shoulder, and my spine stiffened. I didn't need to turn around to know Nix was there, glaring at me.

"What's your problem, Wilder?" Chloe spat.

"Leave it, Clo." Kye joined us, nursing his busted-up hand.

"You should get that looked at," I said.

"Nah." He grinned. "Nothing a little liquor and pussy won't fix."

"Dude, gross." Chloe clutched her throat and pretended to retch.

He turned his attention to her, expression darkening. "I thought I told you not to come tonight."

"And I thought I told you to go fuck yourself."

"I'll tell Mom—"

She let out a bitter laugh. "Seriously? You think I give a crap. She'll be more interested in you getting into another fight."

Kye mashed his lips together at that.

"You know you're one suspension away from getting kicked off the team, right?"

"Don't start, little bit." He leaned over to ruffle her hair, but Chloe swatted him away.

"Don't call me that. I'm sixteen, not a kid."

"Just… go home, Clo."

She snorted. "Whatever, big brother. Come on, Harleigh, let's leave the douchebag brigade to it." She grabbed my arm and tugged me away from them.

They didn't try to stop us.

Nix didn't try to stop me.

Not that I expected him to.

He'd made it pretty clear that he didn't want me here.

But what I couldn't work out was, why?

"SHIT, I'M SO DRUNK." Chloe draped herself over me as we trudged toward some overturned tree trunks away from the chaos.

"Aren't you drunk?" She peeked up at me through her smudged lashes.

"No, I stopped after a couple more beers." When your mom was an alcoholic, it kind of turned you off the whole getting wasted thing.

"Noooo, you need to loosen up. Get drunk and make out with one of those cute zombie football players."

"I think that's your dream, not mine." I chuckled. "Speaking of… he's coming over here."

"Who?" She whipped her head up, almost slipping over the trunk. "Whoa, that was close."

"Clo," Maddox said, looming over us. He was big for a sophomore, already packing some serious muscle.

"Go away, Maddox," she murmured, waving him off.

"Not gonna happen, Clover."

"It's okay," I said. "I'll watch out for her."

"I'm taking her home."

"Like hell you are." She leaped up, getting all up in his face. "You haven't spoken a single word to me all night and now you think you can just swoop in and play hero? Newsflash, buddy." She jabbed her finger in his chest. "I don't want to play your games."

"West," Kye's voice made her bristle. "Take my sister home."

"Don't start, Kye. I've had enough of—"

Maddox bent down and scooped her up, throwing her over his shoulder and stalked off toward the cars littered on the other side of the trees.

"Guess I won't be riding home with Chloe," I mumbled, my fingers curling into the rough bark.

"Come on," Kye said. "Before Nix comes over here and goes all caveman on you too."

Yeah, right.

Like that would ever happen after tonight.

But it wasn't like I had anywhere else to go. With Chloe gone, I was alone.

We walked back to the party in awkward silence. Couples had begun to pair off, hidden in the shadows, pressed close, touching and moaning. Others danced, wild and free, embracing the night of mischief and mayhem.

They made it look so easy, so fun.

It had never felt that way to me. But I was beginning to think that maybe Nix was right. Maybe I was wired wrong.

"What happened earlier—"

"It doesn't matter." Marc Denby was nobody to me. I cared less about the way he manhandled me and more about the way Nix had refused to look at me. As if I disappointed him… *or disgusted him.*

"I think I'm just gonna go," I blurted out, toying nervously with the hem of my cropped tee. I'd felt good leaving the trailer in my Harley Quinn costume. Sexy even. But ever since seeing Nix's reaction, I'd felt like nothing more than a fool.

"Yeah, right. As if Wilder is going to let you leave with some douchebag."

My brows crinkled. After the way Nix had treated me all night, why would he care who I left with?

Kye studied me, his lips quirking. "You two really are clueless sometimes."

"What—"

"Yo, Carter," Zane called. "We're leaving."

"We are?"

"Yeah, got some shit to take care of across town." He flashed us a wolfish smirk.

"Fuck yes. We can drop B off first, right?"

"Yeah, whatever." Nix jumped down off a stack of tires and drained his bottle of water.

He had his own reasons for not drinking. The same way I did.

It was just one of the many things we shared.

"I can try to find another ride home," I said quietly.

Nix went deathly still, inhaling a ragged breath. When his eyes found mine, my heart fluttered wildly in my chest. "You think I'd just leave you here? Alone?"

"I…"

"Come on, Zee man." Kye slung his arm around Zane's neck and started pulling him away. "Let's give B and Wilder some private time."

CHAPTER FIVE

THE AIR CRACKLED AROUND US AS WE STOOD, STARING at one another.

"We should go," Nix gritted out, anger radiating from every pore.

He went to walk off, but I grabbed his arm and cried, "Wait."

His gaze went to where I was holding him before he slowly lifted his eyes to my face.

"Did I… do something wrong?"

God, I hated how weak I sounded, how vulnerable. But I hated this chasm between us.

A chasm he made.

"Harleigh, not here, not now." He let out an exasperated breath.

"What does that even mean? So I have done something? Is it the costume? Because I thought—"

"I can't do this right now." He stalked off, disappearing into the shadows.

Anger bubbled up inside me, exploding like a volcano.

Without thinking, I took off after him. "Don't you dare walk away from me," I shrieked, fists clenched at my sides. "We are talking about this. Right now."

Nix swung around, his eyes shining in the moonlight. "Harleigh—"

"Don't call me that." My heart constricted. "You never call me that."

I was always Wren or Birdie or B.

Him calling me Harleigh felt like an adult scolding a child.

"Just tell me why you're being so… so weird."

Silence stretched out before us, my chest heaving with the weight of the words.

"I…" His eyes darted away, a cuss leaving his lips.

"Phoenix." I stepped forward. "Just talk to me, please." I reached for his hand, but he jerked back.

"Don't."

"I know I'm not like Cherri or—"

"Cherri?" He paled, snorting. "You think this is about Cherri?"

"Well, her… girls like her."

"Birdie, that's not—fuck. Fuck." He thrust his

fingers into his dark hair and pulled the ends, frustration bleeding from him.

"Nix, what's happening to us? I don't—" Nix crowded me against a tree, leaning down and touching his head to mine.

"I…" He stopped himself again and my stomach twisted.

Why couldn't he just talk to me? The way he always had.

"Do you have any idea what you're doing to me?" His voice was a dark whisper in my ear, his lips precariously close to my skin. So close I could feel every word like a gentle caress against my neck.

"M-me?" I asked. Because he wasn't making any sense.

Pressing back into the rough bark, I tried to get a better look at his eyes. It was on the tip of my tongue to beg him to tell me what was wrong. But he curved his hand around my throat, dragging his thumb over my bottom lip.

"So fucking beautiful."

Beautiful?

My eyes grew to saucers as he held me there, pinned against the tree, tracing the shape of my mouth as if I was something precious. Fragile and delicate.

"Nix, w-what are you—"

"Sssh, B. I'm trying really fucking hard not to lose control right now."

It was then I noticed he was trembling. His whole body, shaking as he touched me. It was more than I could ever have hoped for and yet not nearly enough.

"Why," I coaxed. "What would happen if you lost control?"

"This."

Nix's mouth crashed down on mine, hard and demanding. I gasped at the sudden contact as his tongue snaked out, licking my lips.

Oh my God.

Nix was kissing me.

He was kissing me, and it was everything.

Each press of his lips, every stroke of his tongue, took me higher and higher until I was lightheaded, my heart beating so hard I thought I might pass out.

"Do you have any idea how many times I've imagined doing this?" Nix cupped my face, staring down at me, his eyes blown with lust.

"You did?"

A smirk tipped his lips, swollen from kissing me.

"I-I don't understand. Tonight you acted like you were pissed at me."

"I was, Birdie." He nuzzled my neck, sending little shocks through me. "You came out in this ridiculous outfit, looking like sex and sin, and all I could think about was throwing you down and…" He stopped himself, drawing in a ragged breath. "We should go, the others are waiting."

"Go?" I pouted, feeling giddy. "But you were just getting to the good part."

Nix smiled and with that single look, all the tension wrapped around my heart like a fist melted away.

"Come on, little Birdie." He slung his arm around my neck and guided me deeper into the woods, toward where he'd parked his car.

Spotting us, Kye jumped down off Nix's hood. "You two sorted out your differences?" His brow lifted, a knowing smile tugging at his mouth.

"Shut it, asshole." Nix released me and yanked open the passenger door. "B rides shotgun."

"When doesn't she?" Zane grumbled, sliding into the back seat.

"Told you everything was gonna be okay, B." Kye winked before throwing himself inside.

My mouth hung open, confusion swirling in my stomach. They knew… all night they knew what was wrong with Nix. That's why Kye had been making those cryptic statements.

But I still couldn't believe it.

Nix… felt the same.

All this time, and he felt the same about me.

Butterflies soared in my stomach, making me tingle.

Nix backed out of the dirt parking lot with one hand on the wheel and took my hand with his other, flashing me a wolfish grin that did sinful things to my insides. "Ready to cause some mayhem?"

"You're not taking me home?"

"Do you want to go home?" His dark brow lifted, his gray eyes glittering with a challenge we both knew I wouldn't be able to resist.

Pressing my lips together, I shook my head. I didn't want to go home. I wanted to be here with him.

"Good girl." He winked, his eyes darting to my mouth.

Exhaling a long breath, Nix smirked before pulling a U-turn and gunning the engine.

Leaving the party and all my doubts behind us in the dust.

I DIDN'T COME to Old Darling Hill a lot, but I knew the second we crossed the boundary. The houses became bigger, nicer, with neatly mowed lawns and huge sweeping driveways. Flashy cars sat in front of double garages and the streets were adorned with planters and quaint trees.

Old Darling was a quintessential Hudson Valley town, with its idyllic scenery and artisan charm. It was everything Darling Row wasn't. Pretty. Well-loved. Thriving.

"Where are we going?" I asked, brushing my thumb over the back of Nix's hand.

I liked touching him, feeling his fingers twined with mine. It felt intimate. Possessive. And it made the dark parts of my heart sing.

"You didn't really think we'd let Denby walk away without teaching him a lesson, did you?"

"Nix," I whispered. "You can't get into trouble. If Coach Farringdon finds out, he'll—"

"Relax, B," Kye said, leaning forward and draping his arm around the shoulder of my seat. "Coach Farringdon knows he needs us if the Hawks have any shot at making the playoffs."

"Damn straight." Nix grinned at Kye through the rearview mirror. "Besides, we'll be in and out before they ever know we were here."

Nix navigated the streets of Old Darling Hill with ease as I stared out at the houses. Next to the trailers we all called home, they looked palatial. A stark reminder of everything Mom gave up to have me.

How was any of that fair? She'd been cast out of her home, her family, for falling in love with the wrong guy. I'd never really given it much thought before tonight. But it wasn't any wonder that she was lost, drifting through life with nothing but missed chances and bitter regrets plaguing her thoughts.

My sperm donor lived in this neighborhood. At least, I assumed he still did. I wondered if he was home now, with his family—the one he wasn't ashamed to claim as his own.

My chest tightened, but it wasn't hurt, not anymore. I'd long gotten over the idea of having a happy family.

"That's the one," Kye said, pointing to the last house on the row. Set back off the street, it was a beautiful Victorian style house.

"He's back, that's his car."

"Good." Nix held out his hand and Kye dropped his mask into it. "Masks stay on, keep the LEDs off. This place is crawling with security cameras."

He drove past Marc's and followed the street around a slight bend, pulling over. The shadows of the trees lining the sidewalk enveloped the car, secreting it away.

"Stay here, okay," Nix ordered, pulling his hand away.

"No, I'm coming."

"Birdie…"

"Phoenix." I narrowed my eyes, refusing to budge.

"Fine." The corner of his mouth tipped. "You can be our getaway driver. Slide into my seat when we're gone and keep the engine running."

"But—"

"Take it or leave it, but you're fucking crazy if you think I'm going to let you come with us and risk you getting noticed."

"He's right, B. Your costume isn't exactly discreet." Kye smirked and Nix glared at him. If looks could kill, Kye would have been six feet under.

"Fine," I snapped, not liking the tension radiating between the two of them. "I'll be your getaway driver."

Nix's eyes slid to mine, burning with hunger. "That's my girl."

His girl.

He'd called me that so many times before, but it felt different tonight.

"Get the fuck out and wait for me over by the trees," he ordered Kye and Zane.

Kye chuckled darkly, and said, "Watch out, B. He bites when he's hungry."

"Asshole," Zane grunted, shoving Kye toward the

door. They slid on their masks and climbed out, melting into the shadows.

The second the door closed, Nix reached out for me, curving his hand around my neck. He drew me close, his gray eyes pinning me in place. "You good?"

I nodded. "What are you going to do?"

A slow smile tugged at his mouth. "Nothing he doesn't deserve." Nix ran his nose along my jaw, breathing me in. My heart crashed against my rib cage, overwhelmed at his intensity. The air was charged, electrified with the heat simmering between us.

"Be careful," I whispered, knowing there was no point in trying to talk him out of it.

When Nix had his eye set on something, nothing stopped him.

His tongue darted out, running along the seam of my lips, tasting me. A needy whimper spilled out of me as I fisted his hoodie. "Do you have to go?" I smiled. "Zane and Kye could take off and we could…" I trailed off, my cheeks burning with my unspoken words.

Nix drew back, searching my eyes, a pained expression on his face.

"What?" I asked.

"Nothing." He shook his head, the expression

gone so quickly I thought I'd imagined it. "We won't be long. Slide into my seat and wait, okay?"

He hesitated but then murmured something under his breath and climbed out of the car. I crawled over the center console and slid into his seat, running my hands around the steering wheel. I'd passed driver's ed last year, but I couldn't afford a car, so sometimes Nix let me drive his.

I watched them in the rearview as they grabbed something out of the trunk and disappeared down the sidewalk. I'd watched them do a lot of crazy shit over the years, but I'd never been an accomplice before. Nix wouldn't ever allow it. He said my heart was too pure to be tarnished with his degenerate ways. But he was wrong.

Because sitting there in the cover of darkness, waiting for him and the guys to get back at Marc Denby for gate-crashing the party—for putting me in harm's way—my heart didn't race with fear or trepidation.

It beat steady with excitement.

Raw, powerful adrenaline coursing through my veins.

Maybe my mom was right. Maybe Nix had already tarnished me.

Or maybe I really did prefer to live in the darkness, and I just hadn't embraced all that it meant yet.

CHAPTER SIX

NIX OPENED THE DRIVER'S DOOR AND PEERED INSIDE. "Hi," he said, breathless.

The back doors opened and Zane and Kye dove in the back seat, Kye's laughter filling the car. "Holy shit, what a rush," he said, grinning.

"What did you do?" I arched a brow.

"That's for us to know and you to never find out." He winked, and Nix snorted.

My head whipped back to face Nix, but he only smirked. "Better move over, Birdie, or step on it, before the cops show."

My mouth hung open. He wasn't serious, was he?

"Shit, bro, that's cold." Kye leaned over and yanked one of my Harley Quinn pigtails. "Relax, B, no one saw us. But everyone will see Denby tomorrow."

Their laughter washed over me again, making my skin tingle. I'd gone from feeling like the outcast all night to being one of the guys.

And I liked it.

"Seriously though, B, we need to go now. So unless you really want to drive…"

Zane grabbed Kye and yanked him back into the seat as I crawled back over to the passenger seat. "I need to eat."

"Burgers at Pat's?"

"We'll drop you off," Nix said, slamming his door. "Then I'll take Birdie home."

"Oh, I could eat."

I didn't want the night to be over yet.

"It's late. I should get you home," he clipped out and I frowned, my stomach dipping. What the hell was his problem?

We sped off down the street, the wheels screeching as he took the corner.

"Way to be stealthy, asshole," Zane grumbled.

"Blue balls will do that to a guy." Kye snickered and Nix flashed him another dirty look in the rearview mirror.

Surely, he didn't mean…

"Ignore him," Nix murmured as he white-knuckled the steering wheel.

I sank back into the seat, watching the quaint

scenery morph back into the familiar streets. Graffitied street corners and run-down stores. Old, rusted cars discarded outside old houses with chipped paintwork and overgrown lawns.

Sometimes, it was hard to believe our side of town shared a zip code with Old Darling Hill.

By the time we pulled up outside Pat's, the strange uneasiness I'd felt all night had returned, making my stomach churn.

"Fuck yes, I love this place," Kye said. "You sure B can't join—"

"Out," Nix growled.

"Night, B. Hope he goes easy on you."

They slipped into the dark and headed for the diner.

"You're angry again," I said, glancing at Nix.

"I'm not."

"Doesn't seem like it." Sarcasm dripped from my words as I rolled my eyes and folded my arms over my chest. "Fine, just take me home."

His hot and cold act was giving me whiplash.

But Nix didn't take me home.

Instead, he took the road leading away from Darling Row.

"You do know this is the wrong way."

"Harleigh..." He let out a strained sigh.

"I see." I clipped out.

We were back to Harleigh.

My lips pursed as indignation burned through me.

But when he pulled off the main road, down a dirt road, I couldn't deny my curiosity got the better of me.

"What is this place?"

"It's the old grain mill."

"I've never been out here before."

"I come here sometimes. To get away from it all." The car rolled to a stop and Nix cut the engine.

"You know, life won't be like this forever," I said. All my anger toward him dissipating. Because this was my Nix. The boy he didn't let many people see.

"Yeah?" He glanced over at me, a fragile smile playing on his lips. "You think we'll get out of The Row?"

"You don't?"

He shrugged. "Kids like me… they don't get many opportunities, Wren."

"You have football. Coach Farringdon believes you could get a scholarship one day, and so do I. You just have to try to stay out of trouble."

He rolled his eyes. "Don't give me that look."

"What look?"

"You know who I am, B. What runs through my blood. I'm not sure I'm cut out for college."

"His actions don't define you, Nix."

Nix's dad was a mean sonofabitch with a wicked right hook and a penchant for making a quick buck or two no matter how illegal the activity. But he didn't just knock Nix around, he usually took things out on Jessa, Nix's stepmom too.

"You're more than just Joe Wilder's son."

"Maybe. Maybe not." His voice was barely a whisper and there was something so vulnerable about those three little words that my heart cracked.

"Nix, I—"

He snatched my hand up in his and looked me dead in the eye. "I need you to know that it's you, Birdie. It's always been you. But I—"

"No. Don't do this."

Don't end us before we ever got started.

When Nix had kissed me earlier, I'd felt his delirious need for me. The urgency and sheer desperation as his mouth moved against mine. But something had changed in the car. A new fissure in the chasm he'd forced between us.

"Don't you see, Wren. You deserve more than… than what I can give you. So fucking much more."

Strangled laughter crawled up my throat as I tore my hand from his. "I have spent years watching you with girls. Girls like Cherri. Girls who are everything I'm not. Yet, I still want you. I still want you to look at me the way you look at them. I wore this for you, you know?" The words poured out like hot lava. "I wore this so for once, for one night, you'd look at me and see past the image you've formed of me.

"See me, Nix. Please just see me." Tears pricked the corners of my eyes, my heart pounding in my chest.

"I see you, B. I've always fucking seen you, but it doesn't change anything. I'm messed up, baby. Broken and scarred. Those girls are just a means to an end. But you, you'd be my ruin."

A tear broke free. And another. Until a river of tears streamed down my cheeks. He wanted me but he wouldn't let himself have me.

That kiss—my first ever kiss—wasn't the start of something, it was Nix allowing himself one moment. One taste.

"I think you should take me home," I said, unable to look at him.

"Wren, please—"

"No, I can't do this. I need some time."

Because time and distance would help me gain perspective. They would help me see that I deserved more. I deserved someone to meet me halfway.

God, I'd wanted it to be him. But I wouldn't beg.

I was done begging.

"Nix, take me—"

"Stop. Fuck. Just give me a minute okay?"

But I couldn't stop crying. I should have known that one day, Phoenix Wilder would break my heart, but I loved him anyway.

I couldn't *not* love him.

He was my constant. My North Star in dark skies.

But he wasn't mine.

No matter how much I wanted him to be.

"Shit, B, don't cry. Please don't fucking cry."

But the agony in his voice only made me cry harder.

Before I could stop him, he pulled me onto his lap, forcing me to straddle his legs.

"Let me go," I cried, aware of what a mess I was making. Thick mascara streaked down my face, the deluge of tears smudging my Harley Quinn makeup." Just let me—"

"Stubborn girl." He gripped my chin, forcing me to look at him. "You shouldn't give me your tears, Birdie, I don't deserve them."

"You're right, you don't."

"Tell me you'll always be mine. That I'll always own part of this." His hand dropped to my chest, right over my heart.

"No."

"Say it."

I pressed my lips together, shaking my head.

Anger flashed in his eyes, but he managed to calmly say, "Yeah, guess I deserve that. Just promise me, whoever you give it up to will deserve you. Promise me, B."

"Fuck you," I sneered.

He'd ruined everything.

Every-fucking-thing.

And in that moment, I hated him.

His eyes dropped to my mouth and a low groan rumbled in his chest.

"Don't you dare—"

His hand wrapped around my throat as he crashed his mouth down on mine, devouring me. "Need to touch you," he murmured between kisses. "Need to feel you, just once."

Somewhere in the recesses of my mind, a little voice was yelling at me to stop, to not give him anymore of myself. But I couldn't do it.

I couldn't stop him, even if I wanted to... and I didn't.

Because I'd dreamed of this—I'd dreamed for so long of having Nix touch me and kiss me and give me this part of him.

"You taste so fucking good, why do you taste so fucking good?" He trailed hot open-mouthed kisses along my jaw, sucking the skin there, nipping and licking. I shifted closer, feeling him rock hard beneath me. It was so unfamiliar, and yet, so thrilling to know I affected him like this.

Me.

Little Harleigh Maguire.

I rolled my hips, desperate for more friction, overwhelmed at the new sensations rushing through me.

I'd touched myself before. Explored my body under the cover of darkness, alone in my bed. But it had never once felt like this. Like I might die at any second if Nix didn't touch me.

"Keep doing that, B, and this is going to end with me buried deep inside you." He gave me a wicked look, one that said behave.

But instead of heeding his warning, I whispered. "Is that a promise?"

"Fuck," he breathed. "You can't say stuff like that to me."

I could, and I would. Especially if it meant more kissing and touching and just more.

I leaned back in, scraping my nails along his jaw, tracing the seam of his lips with my tongue. Nix bared his teeth, nipping the end of my tongue and then sucking it into his mouth, sending another wave of lust rolling through me. His hands slid down to my ass and he started gently rocking me over him, back and forth, up and down.

"Does that feel good?"

I nodded, trying to trap the whimper building in the back of my throat. It felt too good.

He felt too good.

But it wasn't enough. I wanted more. I wanted him to cure the deep endless ache inside me.

Dipping my head to his neck, I tasted his skin, breathing in his cologne. Clean and male and one hundred percent Nix.

"Touch me," I whispered. "I want you to touch me."

Maybe when the sun came up and the harsh light of day shone down on me, I would regret this moment. But that will be then. This was now.

And right now, I had never wanted anything more than I wanted Nix's hands on my body.

"One night," he said, dousing some of the flames building inside of me. "That's all this can be. Then things go back to how they've always been, Wren."

I nodded, my eyes fluttering as he thrust up against me, our bodies moving in perfect synchrony, as if they knew exactly what to do.

"I'm serious, B." He gripped my chin again, pulling us eye-to-eye. "You're my best friend. My fucking ride-or-die. I can't lose you."

"Stop," I said, attempting to nuzzle his neck again. "Stop making everything so difficult. I want this, I want you."

Even if it's only for tonight.

It would change me, I didn't doubt that. But I had to know—I had to know what it felt like to be with Nix.

He kissed me again, harder, his tongue tangling with mine in deep, demanding strokes. One of his hands slipped around the front of my body and found the slither of skin where my cropped tee ended. My body quivered as he walked his fingers down my stomach, teasing me right below my navel.

"Nix." It came out a breathy plea.

He watched me, his dark-gray eyes pinning me to the spot as he dipped his fingers underneath my skirt and found my panties.

"Fuck," he hissed. "You're soaked."

"For you. Only ever for you." I was mumbling incoherent words, too overwhelmed at the way his fingers stroked me back and forth over my damp panties. It felt divine and he wasn't even really touching me yet.

"More." I lifted my hips, arching into his hand.

"Greedy little thing." He smirked, eyes dark as the night. My heart almost burst when he hooked two fingers inside my underwear and slowly sank them into me.

"Oh God," I cried, anchoring my arms over his shoulders.

"Okay?" he asked, and I nodded. "You're so fucking tight, B." His thumb circled my clit, slow torturous circles that made my eyes roll in the back of my head.

"Never gonna forget this," he rasped, his voice broken with raw lust.

But I didn't want to hear anything that yanked my heart back to earth. Because I was soaring.

In that moment, I wasn't a caged bird, shackled to a dead-end life in Darling Row. I was Phoenix Wilder's Birdie…

And I was free.

CHAPTER SEVEN

Nix was quiet on the ride back to Darling Row. At first, the out of this world feelings had lingered, trickling through my bloodstream like a synthetic high. The way he'd touched me, pushed my body over the edge and made me come undone, it was everything.

But it quickly died when he went back to his closed-off self.

"Nix…"

"Don't, B. Okay." He inhaled a ragged breath. "Just… don't."

"You're making a bigger deal out of this than it is." I clipped out, annoyed that he was ruining every-thing again.

I didn't regret what had happened. Even if he

never touched me again and broke my heart into jagged little pieces, I wouldn't regret it.

"I just finger fucked you in my car." His crass words made me wince. "You're not some whore, B." He threw me a sideways glance, his jaw clenched tight.

"I didn't realize choosing who I let touch me and where, made me a whore."

"That's not what I—" He sighed, scrubbing his jaw. "Forget it. It's late. We can talk about this tomorrow."

"Tomorrow." I snorted. "You mean, when you go back to pretending you don't want me and let girls like Cherri drape themselves over you? Girls who don't care about you. Not the way I do."

"Harleigh—"

"Unbelievable," I shrieked. "Un-fucking-believable. I wanted it, Nix. I wanted to feel your lips on mine, your hands on my body. Because... I. Can't. Stop. Thinking. About. You. I watch you with them and I want it to be me. It should be me." My chest heaved with the weight of the words.

"You're worth so much more—"

"Don't you dare tell me what I'm worth," I yelled. "Do you know what I think? I think you're scared. Because love is messy and hard and it hurts." God, it hurt so much.

"You love me, Birdie?"

"You know I do, asshole."

His lips twisted into a regretful smile. "I wish things were different."

He wasn't going to budge. And I was too emotionally exhausted to try to fight for us tonight. So I pressed my head against the cool glass and watched the familiar rows of trailers roll by.

Darling Row was home. But it had never felt like it.

When we pulled up outside my trailer, the air had turned so thick, I wanted to throw the door open and inhale a lungful of fresh air.

Instead, I turned to Nix and said, "Tomorrow. We'll talk about this tomorrow."

When I wasn't dressed as a second-rate version of Harley Quinn and Nix wasn't shackled by guilt.

He nodded, barely able to look at me.

"Goodnight," I murmured, hesitating. "Whatever you think I deserve, you're wrong. I know my heart, Nix, and it wants you."

With that, I climbed out and didn't look back as I walked up to my trailer. I felt his eyes follow me though, felt his guilt and regret. Convincing Nix to take a chance on us was going to be more difficult than I thought...

But I wasn't going to give up without a fight.

I WOKE UP WITH A START. A sliver of moonlight poured in through the gap in my curtain casting a silvery glow around my small bedroom.

Glancing at the clock, it read three-thirty. I was surprised I'd fallen asleep. When I'd stripped out of my costume and cleaned the makeup off my face, I'd laid on my bed clutching my cell phone waiting for Nix to text me.

But it never came.

The tears did though. Big, fat, ugly sobs that made my soul weary and my heart ache.

Mom had been passed out when I'd checked in on her. Nothing new there. But something had woken me.

Maybe it's him.

I listened, my heart racing in my chest. Did Nix have second thoughts? Did he want to fix things between us?

Throwing back the covers, I tiptoed over to the window and pulled back the curtain slightly. But nobody was out there.

My stomach sank.

Who was I kidding, it wasn't Nix.

Wide awake, I decided to get a glass of water.

Creeping through the trailer, I helped myself to a drink when a strange sensation went through me.

I glanced around, trying to place the unwelcome feeling. "Mom?" I called out, my palms growing clammy.

Padding down the hall toward her room, blood roared between my ears. Something was wrong. I could feel it in the air, dark and foreboding.

"Mom?" I pushed open her door and peeked inside. Relieved to find the outline of her body on the bed.

I went to double back when something stopped me, and I glanced back. "What is—" I slipped inside, hurrying over to her. "Mom?" Reaching out, I touched her cheek, her skin icy cold beneath my fingers. "Mommy?"

Silent tears rolled down my cheeks as realization slammed into me.

My mom was dead.

***

I CLUTCHED my cell phone like a life raft as I sat in Darling Hill's police department. When I'd called 911, they had sent the EMTs along with a police cruiser. I'd been too incoherent to articulate what had happened. Now I was numb.

She was gone.

My mom. The woman who had given up her life of privilege and wealth to have me.

Gone.

Just like that.

Nothing made sense, but part of me hoped she'd found peace.

"Miss Maguire?" The officer with kind eyes approached me. "Your father is here to take you home."

"You must be mistaken," I said flatly. "I don't have a father."

"Harleigh?" The strong, commanding voice washed over me, and I lifted my face to look at its owner. "I'm sorry for your loss," the man said.

"I'm sorry, who are you?" I hugged myself tighter, wanting to be anywhere but here.

What I really wanted was to be with Nix. He would hold me and make everything better. But he hadn't responded to my endless stream of messages. Neither had Kye or Zane when I'd finally caved and texted them too.

Even when I'd left Nix a desperate voice message explaining what had happened, he still hadn't replied.

That had broken something inside me. Something irreparable. Things were strange between us, I knew that. But I needed him, and he wasn't here.

You're all alone now.

"I'm Michael Rowe. Your father."

Bitter laughter spilled out of me as I stared up at the man that was nothing but a stranger. "Like I told the officer, I don't have a father."

"Miss Maguire, your file—"

"My file?" I whipped my head around to the officer in question and frowned. "You have a file on me?"

"Not now," the man claiming to be my father said. "Please, give us some privacy."

"Actually, don't. I have nothing to say to you."

"I came to take you home, Harleigh." He sat down beside me. I hadn't noticed before, but now I could see how immaculately he was dressed.

"I have wanted to meet you for a very long time."

"Don't..." my voice shook. "Don't sweep in here and pretend to care. It's your fault she left Old Darling Hill. Your fault we lived in that shitty trailer. Your fault she couldn't escape her demons."

"I have made mistakes, yes. But I'm hoping to fix—"

"She's dead," I seethed, narrowing my eyes at him. "She's dead and you're sitting here hoping for a do-over."

I saw it then. The resemblance between us. Same jade green eyes and midnight black hair. The slight cleft in our chins.

Michael Rowe was my father.

And he was here to take me away.

"I won't go with you," I said defiantly.

"You're barely seventeen, Harleigh. A minor. If you don't come with me, where will you stay? How will you afford to live?"

"I-I have… friends. They'll help me." I'd been about to say I had Nix, but it had been almost three hours since I'd discovered my mom dead, and he still hadn't replied.

I glanced down at my cell phone again.

Where are you?

"Come home with me and we'll talk about things. I just want to help. You shouldn't be alone right now."

"Mr. Rowe, Miss Maguire, we've processed all the paperwork." A different officer appeared. "You're free to leave."

"Thank you." Michael rose and shook the man's hand. They both stared at me expectantly.

"Do I have to go with him?" I asked.

"You're a minor, Miss Maguire. Do you have another adult you can stay with?"

"I… No." Defeat slammed into me.

"I understand things are confusing and scary right now," he said. "But you're lucky you have family you can stay with."

Lucky.

Nothing about the situation felt lucky.

"Come now, my driver is waiting." Michael motioned for me to follow him. But I was too stuck on the part where he said his driver was waiting.

Who the hell was this guy?

I quickly pulled up a new chat on my cell phone and texted Nix.

Nix, where are you? I need you. A man came to get me. He claims he's my father. He wants to take me home with him. He wants to take me away. Nix… I know things are weird between us, but I need you… please.

But he didn't reply.

Not on the journey back to Michael's house or later that day as I sat in silence at their dinner table pushing food around my plate. He didn't reply that night, when I was alone in my room in a strange new place.

Nix didn't text me.

And just like that, the boy I'd loved my whole life, the boy I thought I could always depend on, became the boy who destroyed me.

82

ABOUT THE AUTHOR

ANGSTY. EDGY. ADDICTIVE ROMANCE

USA Today and *Wall Street Journal* bestselling author of over forty mature young adult and new adult novels, L A is happiest writing the kind of books she loves to read: addictive stories full of teenage angst, tension, twists and turns.

Home is a small town in the middle of England where she currently juggles being a full-time writer with being a mother/referee to two little people. In her spare time (and when she's not camped out in front of the laptop) you'll most likely find L A immersed in a book, escaping the chaos that is life.

L A loves connecting with readers.
The best places to find her are:
www.lacotton.com